For HELGA and PAUL

Yours and Mine

Peter Geißler · Almud Kunert

Translated by Anthea Bell

Frances Lincoln Children's Books

I can pull mine on a string.

Yours is hiding - find the spot!

I can tie mine in a knot.

Yours
keeps
quiet,
still
and
small.

Mine will come back when I call.

Yours behind the door sits tight.

Yours
enjoys
the
rain
and
fog.

Mine has met a funny frog.

Yours
will
eat
roast
chestnuts
soon.

Mine
is
flying
to
the
moon.

Yours
can
read
these
great
big
books.

Mine lurks in corners and in nooks.

Yours fits in a buttonhole.

Mine's
gone
away,
poor
lonesome
soul.

Mine likes music deep or high.

Yours can write its name and spell.

Mine's a secret I won't tell.

Yours and Mine

Mine's big, yours green as leaves in spring.
I can pull mine on a string.

Yours is hiding - find the spot!
I can tie mine in a knot.

Yours keeps quiet, still and small.
Mine will come back when I call.

Yours behind the door sits tight.
Mine goes out for walks at night.

Yours enjoys the rain and fog.
Mine has met a funny frog.

Yours will eat roast chestnuts soon.
Mine is flying to the moon.

Yours can read these great big books.
Mine lurks in corners and in nooks.

Yours fits in a buttonhole.
Mine's gone away, poor lonesome soul.

Yours flies like a butterfly.
Mine likes music deep or high.

Yours can write its name and spell.
Mine's a secret I won't tell.

PETER GEIßLER, born 1962, studied philosophy in Munich where he lives with his wife and son. He writes poetry and works as a journalist and editor. *Yours and Mine* is his first book for children.

ALMUD KUNERT was born in Bayreuth in Germany. She studied painting and graphic design in Munich where she now lives, working as a freelance illustrator.

ANTHEA BELL was born in Suffolk and was educated at Somerville College, Oxford. She is one of the most respected literary translators in the UK. She has been the recipient of a number of translation prizes and awards, among them the 1987 Schlegel Tieck Award for Hans Berman's *The Stone and the Flute* (Viking) and the first Marsh Award for Children's Literature in Translation for Christine Nöstlinger's *A Dog's Life* (Andersen Press). She lives in Cambridge.

Text and illustrations copyright © Carl Hanser Verlag 2000
This edition published in 2005 by Frances Lincoln Children's Books,
4 Torriano Mews, Torriano Avenue, London NW 5 2RZ
www.franceslincoln.com
First published under the title Meins und Deins by
Hanser Verlag, Munich, Germany.

English translation copyright © Anthea Bell 2005

Distributed in the USA by Publishers Group West

British Library Cataloguing in Publication Data available on request

ISBN 1-84507-323-1

Printed in China
9 8 7 6 5 4 3 2 1